Dear Parents:

Congratulations! Your child is taking the first steps on an exciting journey. The destination? Independent reading!

STEP INTO READING® will help your child get there. The program offers five steps to reading success. Each step includes fun stories and colorful art or photographs. In addition to original fiction and books with favorite characters, there are Step into Reading Non-Fiction Readers, Phonics Readers and Boxed Sets, Sticker Readers, and Comic Readers—a complete literacy program with something to interest every child.

Learning to Read, Step by Step!

Ready to Read   Preschool–Kindergarten
• big type and easy words • rhyme and rhythm • picture clues
For children who know the alphabet and are eager to begin reading.

Reading with Help   Preschool–Grade 1
• basic vocabulary • short sentences • simple stories
For children who recognize familiar words and sound out new words with help.

Reading on Your Own   Grades 1–3
• engaging characters • easy-to-follow plots • popular topics
For children who are ready to read on their own.

Reading Paragraphs   Grades 2–3
• challenging vocabulary • short paragraphs • exciting stories
For newly independent readers who read simple sentences with confidence.

Ready for Chapters   Grades 2–4
• chapters • longer paragraphs • full-color art
For children who want to take the plunge into chapter books but still like colorful pictures.

STEP INTO READING® is designed to give every child a successful reading experience. The grade levels are only guides; children will progress through the steps at their own speed, developing confidence in their reading.

Remember, a lifetime love of reading starts with a single step!

Copyright © 2021 Disney Enterprises, Inc. All rights reserved. Published in the United States by Random House Children's Books, a division of Penguin Random House LLC, 1745 Broadway, New York, NY 10019, and in Canada by Penguin Random House Canada Limited, Toronto, in conjunction with Disney Enterprises, Inc.

Step into Reading, Random House, and the Random House colophon are registered trademarks of Penguin Random House LLC.

Visit us on the Web!
StepIntoReading.com
rhcbooks.com

Educators and librarians, for a variety of teaching tools, visit us at RHTeachersLibrarians.com

ISBN 978-0-7364-4179-7 (trade) — ISBN 978-0-7364-9002-3 (lib. bdg.)
ISBN 978-0-7364-4180-3 (ebook)

Printed in the United States of America
10 9 8 7 6 5 4 3

DISNEY
PRINCESS

palace
pets

Ariel's Brave Kitten

by Amy Sky Koster
illustrated by the Disney Storybook Art Team

Random House 🏠 New York

Meet Treasure!

Treasure is a kitten.

She loves the sea!

One day, Treasure climbed
onto Prince Eric's boat.

Treasure took a nap.

The crew found her!

Prince Eric liked

the small kitten!

Treasure helped put flowers on the ship for a special guest.

Princess Ariel
was the guest!
Treasure was excited.

Ariel loved Treasure.

Treasure became Ariel's kitten!

Treasure loves to play
at the beach
with her friends.

They find a boat.

They play in the boat.

A big wave
carries the boat
out to sea!

Treasure is happy.

Her friends are worried.

It starts to rain.

Treasure is scared.

The rain stops.

There is a rainbow!

A wave brings the boat
back to shore.

Eric and Ariel arrive.
They see Treasure
in the boat.
They are glad
the kitten is safe!

Treasure is Ariel's brave kitten!